The Company of CROWS

A Book of Poems

Marilyn Singer

Illustrated by Linda Saport

Clarion Books / New York

Clarion Books
a Houghton Mifflin Company imprint
215 Park Avenue South, New York, NY 10003

Text copyright © 2002 by Marilyn Singer
Illustrations copyright © 2002 by Linda Saport

The illustrations were executed in pastel.
The text was set in 18.5-point Papyrus.

For information about permission to reproduce selections from
this book, write to Permissions, Houghton Mifflin Company,
215 Park Avenue South, New York, NY 10003.

www.houghtonmifflinbooks.com

Printed in Singapore

Library of Congress Cataloging-in-Publication Data
Singer, Marilyn.
The company of crows : a book of poems / by Marilyn Singer ; illustrated by Linda Saport.
p. cm.
Summary: A collection of poems which present various views of crows.
ISBN 0-618-08340-5
1. Crows—Poetry. [1. Crows—Poetry. 2. American poetry.] I. Saport, Linda, ill. II. Title.
PS3569.I546 C66 2002
811'.54—dc21   2001058340

TWP 10 9 8 7 6 5 4 3 2 1

To Quoth the Crow and his company
—M. S.

For Susie Havens, my close friend,
who has very special feelings for crows
—L. S.

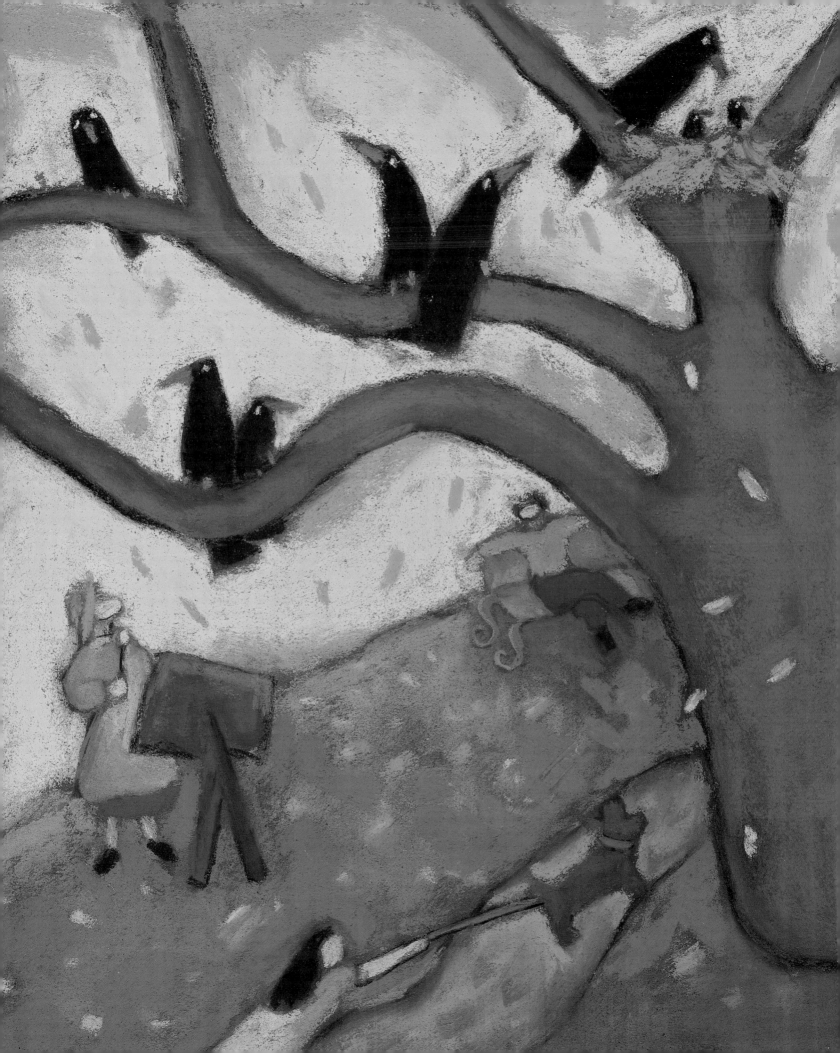

Beak or mind,
Heart or wings,
Crow watchers all
    see different things.
Nest or sky,
Flock or few,
Watching crows have
    their own point of view.

5

"Hello!" he screams
        every day at dawn,
waking the dozy dogs,
        who bark and lunge,
and the napping neighbors,
        who yell, "Shut up, you stupid bird."
Sometimes they even throw stones.
"Hello!" he shouts, unruffled,
        safely settled on the Chasens' chimney
        or the Delmars' satellite dish.
"Somebody better straighten out that fool,"
        my sister grumbles.
"He thinks he's a rooster."
But I think he knows perfectly well
        he's a crow.
And like Jackie Malackey,
        that kid in my class with the fake snake
                and the whoopee cushion
                and the invisible ink,
that bird's just pulling another practical joke
        from his bottomless bag of tricks.

THE GIRL

6

THE YOUNGSTER

Catch the stick
   is a good game
But I know one better:
   Pull the clothespin
I like to watch the white wash
   flutter down
      like gulls' wings
         to the dark ground
Until I hear that girl's mother cry,
   "Oh no! Not again!"
      over and over
Who is she trying to sound like?
It couldn't be
   a crow

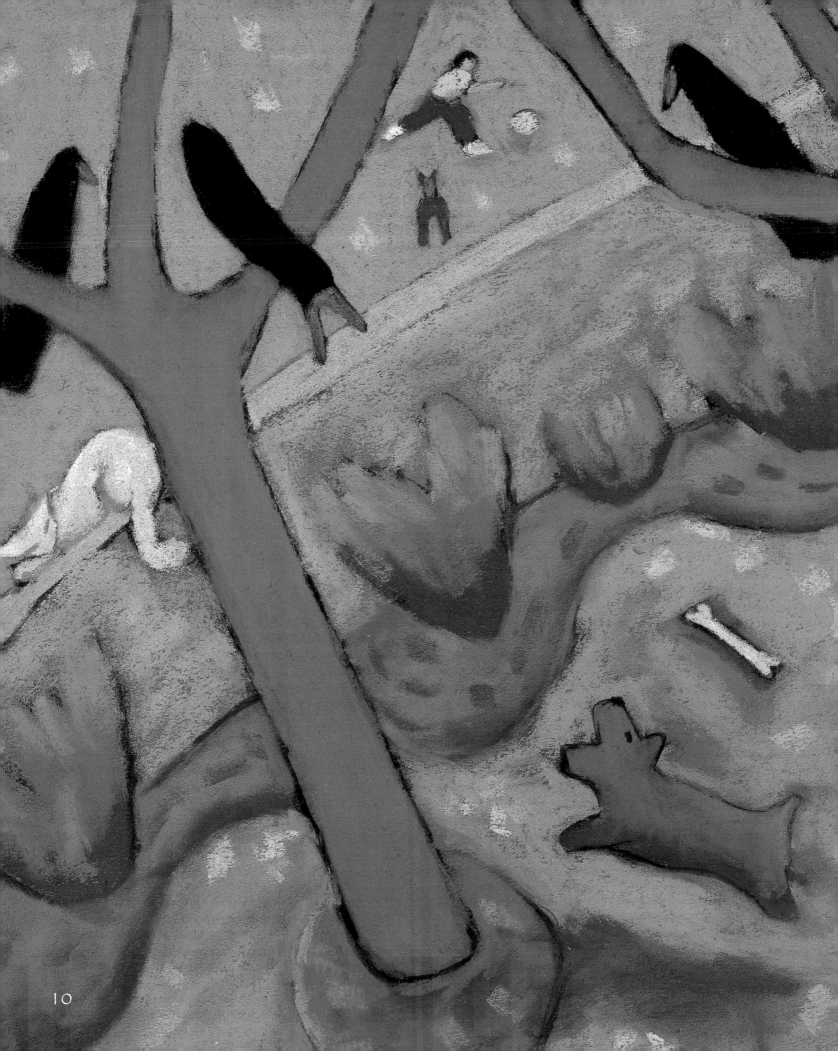

My yard
It's my yard
  My bush
  My grass
  My tree
Everyone knows it—
    That fat purring furball
      sitting on the fence
    That bossy boxer
      from the house next door
    That boy who's always running
    That girl who's always still
My yard
It's my yard
Everyone knows it—
    Except that rude feathered intruder
      squatting on my bush
        my grass
        my tree
    That cackling gate-crashing crow
      always in sight
      always out of reach

THE DOG

It is easy to classify a crow:
   Animal
      with backbone
   Bird
      with feathers
      and beak
   Perches
      on fences
      on limbs
It is easy to identify a crow:
   Feathers
      black and glossy
   Beak
      black and strong
   Eye
      black and keen
   Voice
      a clamor
      a clarion
      a class by itself

THE BIRDWATCHER

It is hard to understand a crow:
What does it think
    in the nest,
    in the skies?
What does it feel
    as it flies,
    when it walks?
When it talks,
    why that voice?
Does a crow have a choice
    how to think, how to be?
Does it wonder
    about its flightless watchers?
Does it ponder,
    who are we?
Or does a crow
    already know?

Quiet—
 they're never quiet
Even at moontime
 they blat and blare and squeal
Peaceful—
 they're rarely peaceful
Even at noontime
 they speed up for a meal
Eating—
 they're always eating
They're always building
 breaking
 cackling quibbling
 hiding finding
 watching
But never sure of what they see.
We have nothing in common
 except fooling, food, and company.
Still, those silly creatures—
 I don't mind
 if they watch me.

THE FATHER

14

THE POET

Winter is a quiet crow
stepping stately, sedately
across a frozen lake.

THE FATHER

Crows like company.
Family breakfasts
   on hot summer mornings,
Neighborly roosting
   on cold winter nights.
Sometimes it is fine to be
   just one
To sail a sweet breeze
To walk a frozen pond
To wander on your own from town to country
   and back again.
But always we return to flocks,
   feasts, and complications.
Leave solitude to woodpeckers,
   hummingbirds, phoebes,
   evil owls, hateful hawks.
We are crows.
And crows like company.

19

THE MOVIE CRITIC

20

Cemetery bird,
  there you are on the big screen,
always sitting on a tombstone
  before the ghouls start to drool.
Or else you're in the desert,
  pecking at a jawbone
where someone's dying of thirst
  or something even worse.
You're on posts near ghostly castles,
You're on gates by weird estates.
You're the messenger of monsters
  on a foggy, haunted heath,
  as the creepy music blares.
What about you always scares us,
  you daytime traveler with no talons,
  you comic dancer with no teeth?
Tell me, how on earth did you get stuck
  as an image of bad luck?

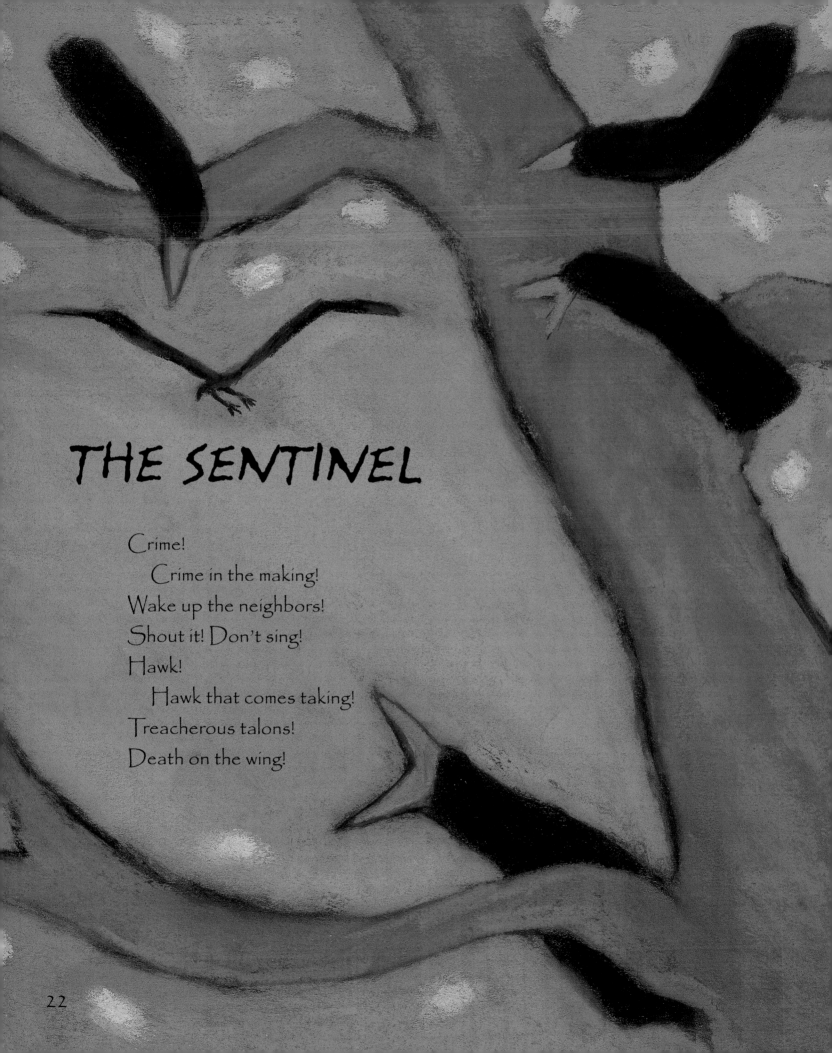

THE SENTINEL

Crime!
   Crime in the making!
Wake up the neighbors!
Shout it! Don't sing!
Hawk!
   Hawk that comes taking!
Treacherous talons!
Death on the wing!

THE TITMOUSE

Oh, the house finch nuthatch black-capped chickadeedle
deedle

I can put up with their pick-peck,
share some berries nuts and seedle
seedle

But that bigmouth bigfoot egg thief crow so greedle
greedle

Can't stand his walk, can't take his talk,
the way he likes to needle
needle

Yet when a sharp-shinned hawk skims by
And crowthroat saves me with a cry

I'm glad he doesn't tweedle
tweedle

23

THE YOUNGSTER

Cranes are not the only dancers
I can do the tail-quiver
  and the quick-step
Come, my friends
Caper with me
  on this fresh-cropped field
Jump out
  Jump back
   Spread each wing like a fan
Dance to greet a partner
  Dance to welcome springtime
Dance because you're merry
  Dance because you can

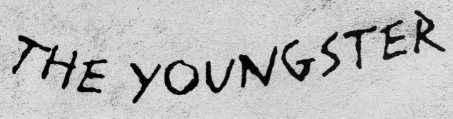

24

I set up a scarecrow
to amuse the crows.
They perch on his tatty straw hat,
his ratty flannel shoulders,
laughing at him,
at me.
But I don't care—
it's part of our pact.
I allow them a lot of laughter
and a little corn.
They rid me of cutworms, caterpillars, grubs,
and self-importance.
Those wheeler-dealers think
they've pulled a fast one.
But me, I say I made the better deal.

THE FARMER

THE PIG

Farmer grunts, Crows can be so annOYING
   True, true
   You can't count on crows
They're always tOYING
    with friends and foes alike
Yet when it comes to emplOYING
    their cheeky beaks
No one's better than
    those back-scratching bug-snatching
    itch-pleasing twitch-easing
    swindlers
whose visit I'm enjOYING

Bow to me
　　my beauty
And say you will allow me
　　to help you build a nest
I swear you'll be impressed

Lean toward me
　　my lovely
And I will let you preen me
　　I'll trust you with my neck
Be gentle—please don't peck

Sport with me
　　my sweeting
I'll court you and you'll court me
　　Together we'll have fun
Two eat better than just one

THE SUITOR

THE MOTHER

Three messy nests my last year's brood
　　are building:
one lopsided
one slopsided
the third half washed away
　　by last night's rain.
I help them by not helping.

Without practice
　　how would they ever learn
the roundness
the tightness
the rightness
　　of a nest?

33

THE BOY

Everyone's baby sister starts with
MaMaDaDaGaGaBo
The right kind of talking,
Real normal, you know?
But my baby sister goes
AwkAwkCahCahUrkUrkCaw
A weird kind of talking
Comes out of her jaw.
It's those big old crows
in the tree near her room,
Preaching and teaching the wrong kind of words—
Unless she's planning on chatting
with a family of birds.

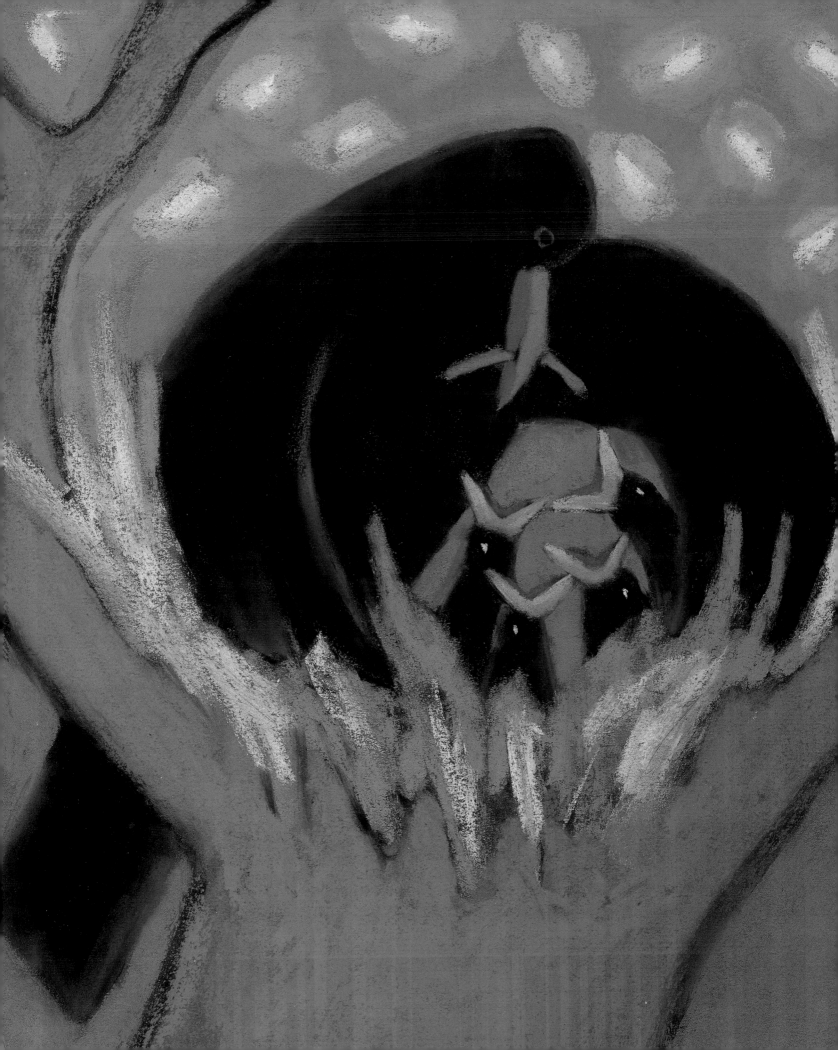

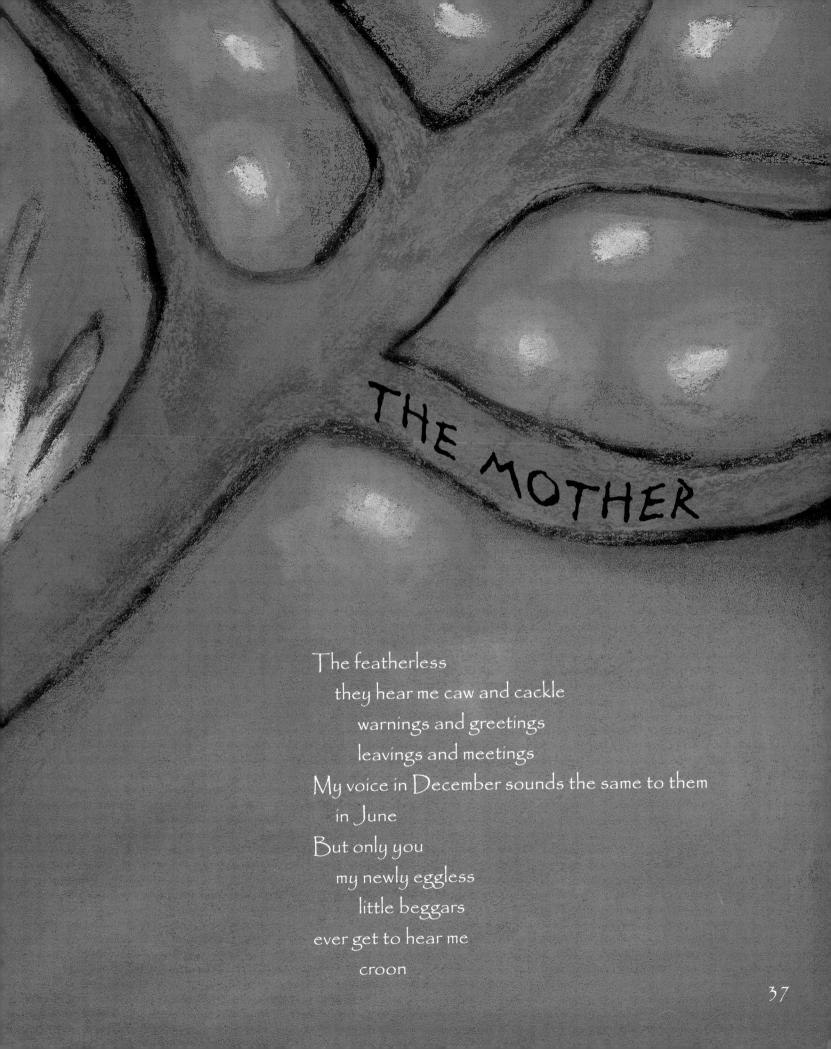

THE MOTHER

The featherless
　　they hear me caw and cackle
　　　　warnings and greetings
　　　　leavings and meetings
My voice in December sounds the same to them
　　in June
But only you
　　my newly eggless
　　　　little beggars
ever get to hear me
　　croon

38

THE PAINTER

You'd think I learned color
 from the cardinal or the goldfinch,
But no—
 I learned it from the crow.
From the blackest wings
 an unexpected rainbow springs,
A sheen of green, purple, blue.
My art is to reveal each elusive hue.
The crow's art is
 to glow.

39

THE BOY

It was the last straw:
    that hammer I borrowed
to build a fort or a clubhouse
    or the crow's nest of a ship
    sailing through a sea of trees.
That hammer missing for just two weeks
Mom found under the underwearshoeboxesseashells
    comicbooksrobotparts
      on my floor.
The last straw, and I had to pay for it,
    doing overtime in my room and the yard.
Outside, muttering mad at the fallen twigsleavesmuck
    I had to rake,
Stuttering bad words at the pair of crows
    ca-ca-cursing back at me,
I found under the mess that wasn't mine
    somebody's shining ring,
      missing for how long, who knows.
Those merry, scolding crows told
    who'd hidden it there,
      but not when.
No matter, new treasure or old—
Like in that story *Rumpelstiltskin*,
The last straw got spun
    into startling gold.

THE MOTHER

My fresh-winged cadets,
    it is time you were leaving
So I'll sing you a song
    on the fine art of thieving
Otters: Tweak their twitching tails
    till they give up their prey
Herons: Just wait patiently
    till their meal slips away
Gulls: Pelt them with some seaweed
    then quickly rob their nest
Robins: If you want their worms
    chasing them works best
Squirrels: Peck their little heads
    then snatch an acorn treat
Turtles: Dig up their tasty eggs—
    use both your beak and feet
Last but not least
    it's important to know:
Do not steal a meal
    from a neighboring crow

THE YOUNGSTER

44

Of course I can get from here to there
    zip
      straight as any crow can fly
But what's my hurry?
There must be time to roll, to flip
    to dive, to dip
to glide instead of flurry
    through the wide and waiting sky

"Goodbye," he caws,
   but he doesn't mean it.
Summer, winter, spring, fall,
   he'll return from the park, the woods,
      the farmer's field,
      wherever it is he goes.
Someplace perhaps a little farther than I've walked
   but no place farther than I'll someday fly.
We're different travelers,
   that bird and I.
I will find myself in places
where I'll greet unfamiliar people
   with *Bonjour, Buenos dias, Konichihwa, Jambo.*
He will always see the same faces.
He will only need to say, "Hello."

THE GIRL

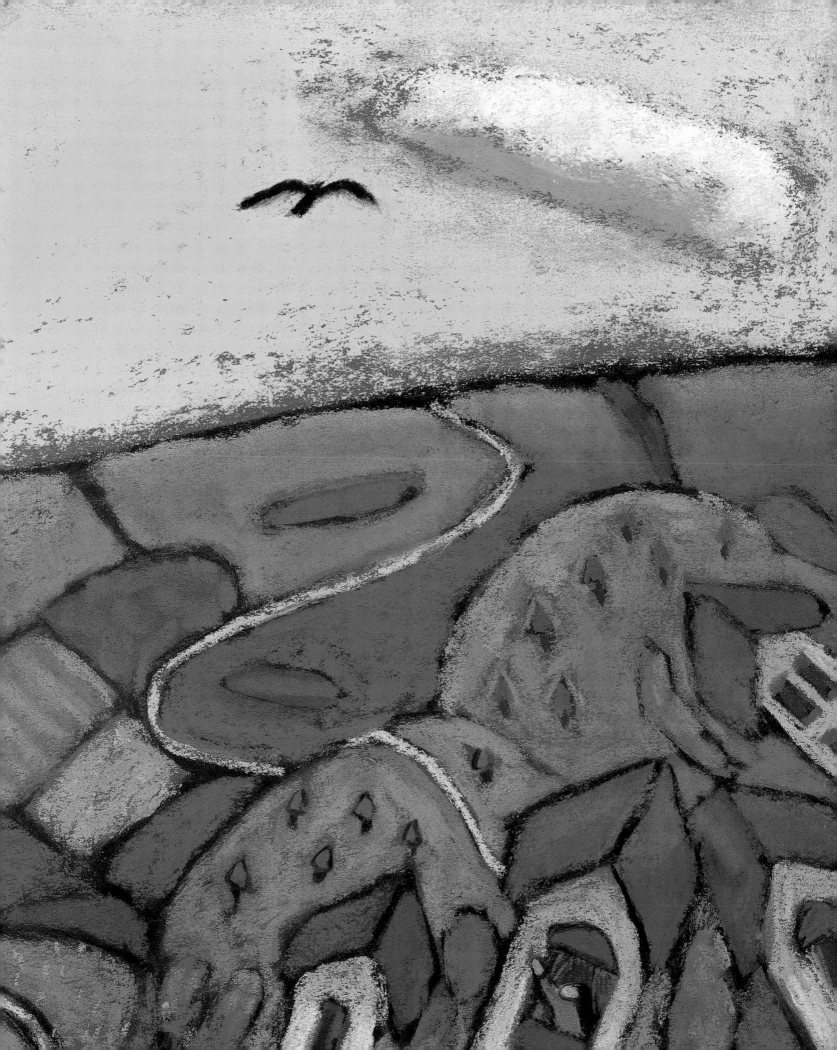

AUTHOR'S NOTE

Many people think of crows as evil birds in scary movies, or as pests that steal farmers' corn. What they don't know is that crows are faithful mates, good parents, and loyal members of their flock. They're also playful, smart, and helpful to the environment.

Crows are social birds. They live in flocks and help each other find food and protect territory. Sentinel crows stand guard to warn their flock of danger. When a sentinel spots a hawk, an owl, or other predator, it will give an alarm cry. Then the flock will mob the predator, cawing loudly and dive-bombing it.

In the fall and winter the flocks are huge. During the spring and summer breeding season, the flocks break up into families. Crow pairs mate for life. Both parents build the nest. The female sits on the eggs, and the male stays nearby to protect them and bring her food. The youngsters born the year before stay with their parents to help take care of the nest and the new chicks.

All crows—especially youngsters—like to play games. They will dance, fly upside down, toss sticks to each other, and get into mischief, such as teasing dogs or pulling clothespins off the clothesline. Crows can solve problems and use tools. Some scientists think they are as intelligent as apes.

It is true that crows will steal corn, hunt animals, and eat carrion. But they will also rid a farmer's field of insect pests or mice that could destroy the whole crop. By eating carrion, they protect people and animals from germs spread by decaying animals.

It's also true that crows are noisy. A crow's caw is loud and harsh. But crows make over twenty other calls, some of which are as soft and gentle as a coo. We rarely hear those calls. They are made to mates and chicks. Crows can also learn to imitate human speech. My pet crow used to wake the neighborhood at dawn with a cheerful "Hello" before he went flying from yard to yard. Then one day, he joined a flock and flew away for good. This book is dedicated to him and his friends.